MURDER
BELOW
ZERO

MURDER
BELOW
ZERO

A MAXINE BENSON MYSTERY

John Lawrence Reynolds

ORCA BOOK PUBLISHERS

M
reynolds

Library and Archives Canada Cataloguing in Publication

Reynolds, John Lawrence, author
Murder below zero : a Maxine Benson mystery / John Lawrence Reynolds.
(Rapid reads)

Issued also in print and electronic formats.
ISBN 978-1-4598-1459-2 (softcover).—ISBN 978-1-4598-1460-8 (pdf).—
ISBN 978-1-4598-1461-5 (epub)

I. Title. II. Series: Rapid reads
PS8585. E94M85 2017   C813'.54   C2017-900837-4
C2017-900838-2

First published in the United States, 2017
Library of Congress Control Number: 2017933367

Summary: Maxine Benson, police chief in a small town, sets out to solve
the murder of the town bully in this work of crime fiction. (RL 3.8)

*Orca Book Publishers is dedicated to preserving the environment and has
printed this book on Forest Stewardship Council® certified paper.*

Orca Book Publishers gratefully acknowledges the support for
its publishing programs provided by the following agencies:
the Government of Canada through the Canada Book Fund and the
Canada Council for the Arts, and the Province of British Columbia
through the BC Arts Council and the Book Publishing Tax Credit.

Cover design by Jenn Playford
Cover photography by Getty Images

ORCA BOOK PUBLISHERS
www.orcabook.com

Printed and bound in Canada.

20 19 18 17 • 4 3 2 1

For Jill and Ian

ONE

"You wouldn't be upset if this were January," Margie Burns said.

"I wouldn't be upset if this were Baffin Island either," Maxine Benson said. "But it's not. It's June in Muskoka, and I have to wear a sweater, which is wrong. All wrong."

It was early on a Monday morning, just past seven.

"I hear we might get more frost tonight," Henry Wojak said. He wrapped his hands around his mug of coffee, cradling the warmth.

Winter had been mild and almost free of snow. Everyone looked forward to a soft spring and a hot summer. *That's the way it works around here*, they said. *Shiver in January, swelter in June.*

March was sunny and mild, April was soft and showery, and May was as fine as a May could be. June, people believed, would kick off a warm and sunny summer.

This was good news for Port Ainslie. Its economy depended on tourists, who came to swim, sail, golf and water-ski. Warm summer days brought crowds who dined and shopped, taking memories and leaving money behind. Lots of money. One spell of bad weather in spring could cancel their plans to visit the "Home of Muskoka Magic," as the town called itself.

But there was no magic to frosted windows in June.

Summer was staying away, and so were the tourists. On the second morning in June, snow fell on top of Granite Mountain and lawns shone with frost. *It's just a cold snap*, people said. *It'll be gone soon.* But now it was the middle of June, and the cold remained. People began saying to each other, *Tell me again about global warming... I could use a laugh.*

"These things happen," Margie said. "The weather has its own mind, you know. We just have to give it time."

"I'd like to give it hell," Henry said. He had finished his coffee and was blowing into his cupped hands.

"Well, you must admit," Margie said, "people behave themselves in this weather. Makes our job easier. If things get slower around here, we'll all have to retire." She was making her weekly report to town council on crime in Port Ainslie. There was never much to tell, but this week there was even less than usual. Margie looked over the list again.

Bruce Olivier Pratt Chadwick, known as Bop, had spent Tuesday night in a jail cell for being drunk in a public place.

The truth was, he had been sober. It would have been too cold for Bop to sleep in the park that night, so he had asked Margie to let him sleep in the corner cell, his favorite. Margie said she couldn't do it unless she booked him for a crime. Bop swore he was drunk, so Margie said okay and asked how he would like his eggs in the morning.

There had been a break-in at a cottage down the lake, but the owners said nothing was taken. A power generator had been stolen from a home on Creek Road. Max had to tell a teenage rock band to close the garage door when they were playing. Even with the door closed they were loud, but no one seemed to care. A dog had run through the town without a leash. Everyone knew the dog's owner was old Dale Carter, so Max had called and told him where to find his dog. *Take it home and keep it tied up*, she said. Carter felt so guilty that he sent Max a box of chocolates for her trouble.

And early in the week a woman had called to report her husband missing. He had been gone two days. His name, she said, was Robert Morton. Max had passed this on to the Ontario Provincial Police, who handled serious crimes. A missing person was serious, but Max knew that most missing people turned up within a few days. She and Henry and Margie dealt with small matters. Like unleashed dogs, petty theft and loud bands.

"Less trouble than normal this week, thanks to the cold weather," Margie said. She closed the report book. "I swear they have more crime over at the St. Mark's bridge club."

Max and Henry stood looking out the window. They had finished their morning chat. Now there was not much to do but watch people pass by on Main Street. Most wore winter jackets, scarves, hats and gloves.

"Geegee offered to help me paint my kitchen cupboards," Max said. Geegee was Gillian Gallup, Max's next-door neighbor at Willow Cove, west of town. Gillian's husband, Cliff, ran a music store and gave guitar lessons to boys who dreamed of being the next Eric Clapton. "I thought I'd wait until the fall to do it. Maybe this would be a good day to start."

"What color?" Henry asked.

Henry liked to know details about everything.

"Color?" Max said. She turned to frown at Henry.

"Your kitchen cupboards," Henry said. He stared at her like a man waiting to hear if his lottery ticket had the winning number.

"I was thinking…," Max began.

Which is when the phone rang.

Max hit the phone's speaker button and said, "Port Ainslie Police Department,

Chief Benson here." Max liked to say her title. She was the only female police chief in Muskoka, and she wanted everyone to know it.

A woman's panicky voice sounded from the phone's speaker. "There's…," she began. She started over. "There is a man lying in the ditch on Bridge Road, near Elm Street."

Where, Max wondered, was Bop Chadwick? "Is he drunk?" she asked.

"I don't know," the woman said. Her voice was lower and more steady now. "I mean, he is naked. And dead. And it looks like he's frozen stiff."

"If this is someone's idea of a joke about the weather," Margie said while Max and Henry grabbed their jackets and ran for the door, "they have gone too far."

The door slammed and the sirens began as the cruisers pulled away, heading for Bridge Road.

"Much too far."

It was on a lonely stretch of Bridge Road, just before the road curved down to Main Street. The ditch was deep, carved by rushing water over the years. A dozen or more cars could have passed since sunup without any of the drivers seeing the body. Someone had covered it with a blanket.

A group of people stood across the road, whispering among themselves. Max told Henry to set up roadblocks and keep traffic on the far side of Bridge Road. Then she stepped into the ditch and lifted the blanket from the body.

The man was indeed naked and, she guessed, between thirty-five and forty years of age. His legs were pulled up so that his knees almost reached his chest. Max reached to touch the body with her finger. It felt frozen. She bent to have a close look at his neck. Raw red marks told her he had been choked to death with a rope or cord. There was a half-moon scar under his right eye.

Stepping out of the ditch, she looked up and down Bridge Road, then back at the body. The man, she was sure, had been dumped from a car into the ditch. The car must have stopped, but there was no way to get a copy of the tire tracks now. They were covered by the footprints of people who had come to look at the body.

Max called Henry over. "Take the names of everyone here," she said. Then she walked to her cruiser, called Margie and told her to call the OPP in Cranston. "Tell them we have a murder here," she said. "Have them send a team to take the body to the morgue." Then she said, "Tell me about the missing-person call that came in last week."

She listened to Margie read from the report.

"By the sound of things," Max said when Maggie finished, "he is no longer missing. He's in a ditch on Bridge Road, dead as a duck and frozen like a Popsicle."

TWO

"**Y**ou're sure you didn't touch a thing?"

The OPP officer had not bothered to give Max his name. He just nodded as he walked past her and knelt next to the body. Max had time to read the name on his tunic. Boucher. When Max didn't reply, he turned to look at her with a glare.

He's treating me like I'm a suspect, Max thought. "My name is Benson," she said. "Police Chief Maxine Benson. I head the force here."

Boucher threw her a cold smile, and his body jerked with a short laugh. "*Chief*?" he said. "Really? And this is your force, right?" He stood and waved a hand toward Henry, who was holding back the crowd. A white van marked *Coroner* was arriving. "You and him are the whole force, I'll bet."

Max was about to say, "And Margie," but the OPP cop wanted to talk.

"You know, this town," he said, nodding toward Main Street, "this town should do what all the towns around here do. It should leave things to us. You shouldn't even have answered the call about this body. So don't try to play detective, okay? You'll just get in the way."

Max told herself to stay calm. "The body has not been moved or touched," she said. "The blanket came from the woman who found the body."

"Where is she?" Boucher looked around, his hands on his hips.

Max turned and pointed. "She's in the black coat over by…"

"You need to get her name, address, details…"

"I have them." Max showed him the notebook in her hand. "I'll have it typed and sent to you." She turned at the sound of a car behind her. A second OPP cruiser pulled to a stop. Two more OPP men stepped out and walked to the body. They stood looking around as though the killer might be standing on the road or in the woods beyond it.

"Bert, talk to that woman over there in the black coat," Boucher said to one of the men. "She found the body." To the other officer he said, "Do a walk around. Make sure the scene is secure, then set up a tent to hide the remains." He turned to Max. "Ma'am," he said, "would you mind stepping aside to make room for Dr. Yates?"

A white-haired man smiled as he stepped past her to reach the body. Boucher pulled a notebook from his tunic and began writing in it.

"I may have a name for the victim," Max said.

Boucher kept writing, acting like he hadn't heard her.

"He matches a person reported to us as missing," Max said.

Boucher was still writing. The coroner moved one of the dead man's arms.

"I can give you the details," Max said.

Boucher did not look up from his notes. "If you have already informed us, as you should have," he said, "we will have it on hand in Cranston. Now could you move away, please? I need a clear view down this road." He nodded toward Henry. "You could go and help your partner over there handle traffic."

Max walked to her cruiser and drove away, making the tires squeal as she left.

"Then he told me to help Henry direct traffic," Max said to Margie. It was half an hour later. Max walked back and forth in front of Margie's desk while she spoke. Her face was still red with anger.

"Did you tell him you were the police chief here?" Margie said.

"Of course I did," Max said. "He made a joke of it. Said he and the two guys with him outnumbered us. That's when I came back here." She took a copy of the missing-person report into her office and closed the door.

She knew all she needed to know about the OPP officers who had treated her like a child. Now she wanted to know about the frozen victim who, she assumed, was the man reported missing a week ago.

Robert Ross Morton had been thirty-seven years old and married to Beth Morton, the former Beth Higgs. He had thin dark hair and a small scar under one eye. Max had seen that scar. This was the man in the ditch on Bridge Road.

The OPP had done a trace on the missing man. Their report had arrived two days ago and said that Morton once worked for a new-car dealership in Toronto. He had lived in Don Mills with a wife and two children. Three years ago he had left his family, filed for divorce and moved to Port Ainslie, where he married Beth Higgs. The widow Higgs's first husband had drowned in their swimming pool earlier that same year.

Max thought, She lost two husbands in three years? Is that just bad luck?

When Bob Morton and Beth Higgs married, he began working for a car dealership in Cranston. He and Beth shared a home on Sunset Hill, one of the richest areas of Port Ainslie. The house had belonged to her first husband, Frank Higgs.

Beth Morton had called a week ago to report her husband missing. She had not seen him since they argued on Saturday night. That's when Morton had left the house, telling her he needed time "to think things over" concerning their marriage. He had walked away, leaving their car in the garage. She went to bed, waking in the morning to find he had not returned. When he was not back on Monday morning, she reported him missing.

The body in the ditch on Bridge Road was Bob Morton. Max had no doubt about it. He had been choked to death with a rope or cord before being folded into a freezer.

Find the freezer, Max thought, and we find the killer.

If only things were that easy.

Margie leaned into Max's office. "Someone is here to see you," she said. She lowered her voice and raised her eyebrows. "A good-looking man in a uniform." She took a step into Max's office and placed a card on her desk.

The card read *Ronald A. Boucher, Provincial Constable 1st Class, Ontario Provincial Police*. Max stepped out of her office and noticed that Constable Ronald A. Boucher had deep-blue eyes. He still had the same cold manner, however.

"The remains are on their way to Cranston," he said. No greeting, no handshake. "Based on what we know at the moment, the victim may be the person in the report you sent to us last week. His name was Robert Morton. We will send you the coroner's report, if you wish."

Max's anger boiled over. "Damn right I wish," she said. "The body was found here, and he is a citizen of this town. Why would I *not* be interested?"

To her surprise, Max's small tantrum seemed to impress Boucher. "Of course," he said. "I will see that you get a full report."

"How did his wife react to the news?"

Boucher, who had turned to leave, stopped to look back at her. "Who?"

"The victim's widow. Her name is Beth. How did she take the news that her husband was found naked and frozen stiff in a ditch?"

"We don't know." Boucher did not look pleased. "A female officer is on her way from Cranston to tell the spouse. It's best to have a female officer break this kind of news to a..." He looked for the word. "A wife."

"Tell her to turn around and go back," Max said.

"Who?"

"The female officer."

"Why?"

"Because this is my case, and I have twenty years of doing that kind of thing in the big city," Max said. "Those are two reasons. Do you want a third?"

Boucher smiled at that. It was a nice smile. Cold but nice. Max might have stayed to enjoy it more, but she brushed past Boucher on her way to Margie's desk. "Call Henry from Bridge Road," she said to Margie, "and put him on patrol." She looked back at Boucher. "You didn't ask," she said.

Boucher blinked. "Ask what?"

"The third reason. It's because the wife and I are the same gender." She walked back to her office.

"Just break the news to her," Boucher called to her back. "Tell her she needs to come to Cranston and view the body. Be sure not to ask any key questions or reveal any facts."

In your dreams, Max said to herself. She grabbed the keys to the *Port Ainslie Police Chief* car from her desk.

She would handle this her way.

THREE

Most people who built their dream home in Port Ainslie chose to build it on Sunset Hill. The Hill, as everyone in town called it, gave those who lived there a perfect view of Granite Lake. On summer nights, folks on The Hill could sit on their patios and watch the sun set over the lake. It was a million-dollar view for people with a million dollars to spend on it.

Beth Morton's house was near the top of The Hill, with large windows over-looking the lake. Pressing the doorbell, Max turned to admire the view. She was still gazing at it when the door opened and a woman's voice said, "Yes?"

The woman at the door looked like a movie star ready for a camera to capture her fading beauty. Her makeup showed off her large green eyes, and her blond hair was set in loose curls. She wore a pink sweater, a tight black skirt and high-heeled shoes. "May I help you?" she said.

"Are you Beth Morton?" Max said.

"Yes. What can I do for you?" Beth Morton's smile did not change. She held her left hand near her face, giving Max a view of her large diamond ring.

Max showed the woman her badge. "May I come in for a moment?"

"Why, of course," Beth said with the same voice and same fixed smile. How many women, Max thought, greet a police officer at their door as though they are being asked to buy Girl Guide cookies? She followed the woman into the house.

Looking around, Max thought she could have been in a high-priced furniture store. Every chair, table and rug appeared new and matched one another perfectly. To Max, it said more about the owner's wealth than about her taste.

One thing in the room stood out from the rest. It was a large oil painting that hung above the sofa. The painting was in a modern style that Max usually did not like. But this one worked for her. The colors flowed into each other in a way that pleased the eye yet also gave a sense of power. Max had to force herself to look away from it when she spoke. She turned to the other woman and said, "I'm afraid I have some bad news for you."

Beth's smile faded only a little. "Really?" she said. "What would that be?"

"The body of a man who may be your husband was found on Bridge Road this morning."

Beth moved her hand to her mouth and said, "Do you think it's Bob?"

Max said, "Yes, I do. We need you to view the body. Are you able to do that?"

"Do I have to?" Beth said. "This is such a shock, and I don't know if I could bear to look at a dead body. I mean, of my husband. It sounds so…" She turned away and brought her hand to her eyes.

Beth Morton, Max thought, had style and a good sense of fashion.

But she could use some acting lessons.

She might even think to ask how her husband had died.

———

"Do you mind if I don't speak much on the way?" Beth said. "I'm quite upset." Seated next to Max in the police car, she had yet to act like a woman who had just been told her husband was dead. She was busy filing her nails.

"I would like to ask a few questions," Max said.

Without looking up, Beth said, "Go ahead."

"When was the last time you saw your husband?"

"I told you. The Saturday before I called. So that makes it just over a week ago."

"You said you had argued before he left."

"Correct." Beth put the nail file in her purse and looked out the window.

"Over what?"

Beth turned away from the lake to look at Max. "Oh, the usual things that a husband and wife talk about. You know."

"No, I don't know." Max glanced at the woman. "Can you tell me more?"

Beth raised a hand to pat the back of her hair. "Bob had a jealous streak. He thought every man who smiled at me wanted to whisk me off somewhere. To bed, mostly."

"Is that what the fight was about?"

"And other things. Mainly that."

"Who was the man who made him jealous that night?"

"No one. It was always no one. Bob would make up someone and say I wanted to be with that person. He wanted to start a fight. He always wanted to start a fight after he drank too much."

"Did he ever hit you or say that he might?"

Beth took more time to answer than Max thought she needed. "I prefer not to talk about it."

She wants me to think she meant yes, Max thought.

They'd driven through the town and were on the road to Cranston when Max said, "Your husband worked for a car dealer, is that right?"

"Yes, that was his work," Beth said. "Or trade. Whatever you call it."

"That's a very nice house you live in."

Beth looked at Max. "So you wonder how I can afford to live there?"

"Well, I was just…"

"My first husband worked in stocks and bonds." Beth still sounded bored. "He was very good at it. He made a lot of money for himself and for his clients. People who come up from Toronto to spend the summer here got to know him. They paid him to look after their assets. He made lots of money for them, and they made lots of money for him." She looked down at her nails. "His name was Frank Higgs, and he drowned in our pool. It was very sad. He left me his estate, including the house." She looked at Max as though Max had insulted her. "So that is how I am able to live in such a nice house. Many people envy me for that." She patted the back of her hair again. "And other things."

Isn't it strange, Max thought, that she felt she had to tell me how her first husband died.

They drove in silence the rest of the way. Max would have liked to ask more questions. But she was happy not to say another word to Beth Morton. For a while.

———

They were in luck. The lift bridge between Port Ainslie and Cranston was not up to let boats on the river sail under it. This happened every half hour in summer months, even a cold summer month like this one. Sometimes the old bridge would get stuck when it was up, and it would take hours to lower it. Meanwhile, traffic would back up in both directions. Not today.

The morgue was at the back of the OPP station in Cranston. Max found a spot to park the cruiser and led Beth inside. "Please tell Constable Boucher we are here," she said to the attendant. Then she asked to see the body of Robert Morton.

The attendant did not ask if they wished to view the body by video. He took both women into the viewing room, where Robert Morton was on a table under a plain white sheet. The body had thawed enough for the legs to be stretched out.

Max watched Beth as the attendant pulled the sheet from the face.

Beth blinked twice and nodded. "That's him. That's my husband." She turned to Max. "Can we go now?"

Boucher found them in the hall on their way out of the morgue. "I would like to speak to Mrs. Morton for a moment," he said to Max. His voice told Max he did not want to debate things. Taking Beth's arm, he said, "Excuse us," turned and was gone.

Less than five minutes later he was back, alone. His face was red, and he looked stern. "The victim's wife told me you grilled her on the way here," he said. "You were told not to do that."

"I did not *grill* her," Max said. "I asked her to tell me a few things. A *very* few things. That is my right. I am an officer of the law, and the crime took place in my area."

"You do *not* have a right," Boucher said. He sounded like a grade-school teacher speaking to a naughty child. "Only the OPP is qualified to question citizens on a matter like this. I am asking you to leave now. I will take Mrs. Morton home."

"She came with me and she will go back with me." Max rose to her full height, which brought her up to Boucher's chin.

"You are out of your league," Boucher said.

"*And you're out of line!*" Max spat back at him.

Two OPP men passing in the hall stopped to watch and listen. Boucher did not want an audience. He turned his back to them and lowered his voice. "I will send you my first report on this case later today," he said. "If you wish to see it. But she is staying here to make a formal statement. Is that clear?"

Max knew she was beaten. The OPP indeed had the power to take over a murder case. But she would not give in without a fight. "I don't *wish* to see that report," she said. "I *demand* it."

Then she left.

FOUR

"The OPP think they are the only ones who can enforce the law," Max said. It was more than an hour since she had returned from Cranston, and she was still angry. She had her feet on her desk and a mug of Margie's coffee in her hand.

Margie stood in the doorway, nodding her head at Max's words.

"That's how cops like Boucher throw their weight around," Max went on. "You and I and Henry, we know people here. We see them every day. They pay our salary...they know we care." She looked out the window and frowned. "This guy doesn't know them or the town and doesn't care. He doesn't know me either and cares even less. I mean, why can't…"

Max looked up to see that Margie was no longer in the doorway. From down the hall came the sound of a printer. A moment later Margie was back at the entrance to Max's office.

"His report came in," Margie said. "I printed a copy for you." Margie held a sheet of paper toward Max.

"The OPP wants to do it all by the book," Max said. She took her feet off the desk and reached for the report. "They won't look at things that don't seem to fit. That's what good cops do. Good cops find things that guys like Boucher never see." She began to read the report.

"You must admit he's a good-looking devil," Margie said.

Max's head snapped up. "Who?"

"Constable Boucher." Margie stepped back and leaned against the doorjamb.

"Writes a pretty good report too, from what I could see." She nodded at the paper in Max's hand. "Read it for yourself."

Max read it.

SUBJECT: Robert H. Morton

1. *Deceased died due to being strangled. The cord or rope was of 10 mm width.*

2. *Death took place 8 to 10 days before body was found.*

3. *Remains were kept below 0° C for a period of time.*

4. *Deceased had a blood alcohol level of 0.18 percent at time of death.*

5. *Spouse of deceased claims he left home around 8 PM nine days before body was found. This followed an argument between her and the deceased.*

6. *Spouse of deceased made Missing Persons report to Port Ainslie P.D. two days later. No response noted.*

7. *Interviews of neighbors reveal presence of male, 25 to 30 years of age, run in*

and around residence prior to deceased reported missing. Ms. Morton confirms male was her brother, one Stephen Edward Carson, age 31, no fixed address. Height: 175-180 cm. Weight: 70 kg. Hair: blond. Eyes: Gray.

8. *Carson drives a black Ford F-150 pickup, year and license unknown.*

9. *Ms. Morton does not know where Carson or the vehicle can be found. She claims he left her house prior to the argument with the deceased.*

10. *Carson is a person of interest.*

Ms. Morton was returned to her home at 15:25 in the company of Constable Wendy Kormos.

R. Boucher PC 1st Class

Max snorted and shook her head. She was angry at the claim that Beth Morton had not received a response from Port Ainslie police after reporting her husband missing.

She tossed the paper aside. "He calls this a report?" she almost shouted. "I've had shopping lists longer than this!"

"You're upset that he talked to that woman, aren't you?" Margie said. "The victim's wife. And he got her story instead of you."

"Of course I am," Max began.

"But that's the deal, isn't it? We look and report, they question and charge." Margie meant the deal with the OPP.

"I know that." Max folded her arms. "It's just that I'm not used to it. We can question and charge as well as they can. Maybe better."

Margie watched her over the top of her glasses.

"I know, I know," Max said. "I had better get used to it."

Margie nodded and smiled.

"But they're not the only ones who can ask questions, right?" Max slid her feet out from under her desk and reached for the keys to her police car. "I mean, what's this about some long-lost brother? Where did he come from? And where did he go?"

Before Margie could speak, Max had her cap on her head and was out the door. "Find Henry," she called as she left. "Tell him I'm up on Sunset Hill and he's to stay on patrol until I get back."

———

"I would like to talk to you about your brother," Max said when Beth Morton answered her door.

"I spoke about Steve to the OPP," Beth Morton said. She had changed into a black sweater and black leggings. "I don't know why you're here to ask more questions."

"It will take just a minute or two," Max said.

Beth shrugged. "All right, I guess," she said. She stepped aside for Max to come in. "I don't mix much with my neighbors. We don't have a lot in common. It's good to have company. Even if it's the police. Would you like some hot coffee?" She wrapped her arms around her chest. "I swear, if things don't warm up soon I'll go to Florida for the rest of the year."

"I'll pass on the coffee," Max said. She walked into the living room. Leaving the country during an investigation into the murder of your spouse was not a good idea. Max thought about telling Beth this, but decided to stay silent. Instead she said, "Do you own a freezer?"

Beth tilted her head like she was being patient with a child. "Are you serious?"

"Yes," Max said. "I am quite serious."

"You mean a freezer big enough to hold a man's body."

"That's right."

"Because you think I was involved in Bob's murder." A statement, not a question.

"That's not the point," Max said. Which was a lie. Max was sure Beth knew more about her husband's death than she was telling. Much more. "I am just looking to rule out a few things, that's all."

"Well, you can rule this one out. I do not have a freezer larger than the one in my refrigerator. You are welcome to look at it or anywhere else if you like. Just bring a warrant with you. And the idea that I would keep a body in my home, my husband's body, is..." She shook her head, looked away and covered her eyes.

Max started over. "Tell me about your brother."

Beth dropped the hand from her eyes. "I told that to the OPP officer."

"But you didn't tell me your brother was here when you and your husband argued. The night that he left."

"It didn't seem important. He left before the argument started."

Max said nothing.

"I see Stephen now and then," Beth said. She sat in a wing chair and looked at Max, then away. "He's a free spirit. All messed up, but gifted. A very good artist, by the way. He did that work over there." She pointed to the painting that had caught Max's eye on her first visit. "Gave it to me years ago. I've come close to burning it."

"Why?"

"Because it reminds me of him, and he drives me mad. He is so hard to get along with. Sweet one minute, full of rage the next. He was a strange kid who grew into a strange adult. We don't get along. Never did. He thinks I'm selfish, and I think he's immature. Never has a home. One day he's in Europe, the next day he sends me a card from Asia. When he is down and out with nowhere else to go, he shows up here for a place to sleep. Then he's gone and I don't hear from him for a year or more."

"When did he come here last?"

"Two, three weeks ago."

"How did your husband get on with him?"

"They put up with each other. That's all." Beth rose from the sofa. "Excuse me," she said. "If you don't want coffee, I do." She walked toward the kitchen, then paused and looked back. "You're welcome to come and see my freezer if you like," she said with a cold smile. "It's on the top of the fridge."

"Thanks," Max said. "I have just a few more questions to ask, if you don't mind." She waited until she could hear water running in the kitchen. Then she walked to the painting. She lifted a corner and looked behind the frame at a small label that read *Elendt Gallery...Home of Great Canadian Artists.* Below it was a Toronto address and phone number.

She set the painting back in position and then walked to the kitchen. Beth was filling a coffeemaker with water. "I think I'll be going now," Max said. "Thanks for the offer of coffee. I can see myself out."

Beth shrugged and said, "Suit yourself."

Outside, the air seemed to have grown colder now that the sun was about to set. Max didn't feel the chill. She had a clue she was sure Boucher did not have. She just wasn't sure what to do with it.

FIVE

Geegee bought tea through a source on the Internet. It seemed to Max a strange way to buy tea. Still, Geegee's tea was always good. "They must have a hundred flavors," Geegee had just told Max. "Some are strange, but this one is great."

Max agreed. She needed coffee in the morning and enjoyed a decent wine with a meal now and then. But nothing made her feel better at night than a cup of tea. Like the one she sipped now in Geegee's kitchen. Geegee called it a country kitchen. It was large, with a stone fireplace, and filled with Quebec pine furniture. "What flavor is this?" Max asked.

"Cream Earl Grey," Geegee said. "How about some shortbread to go with it?"

Of all the things Max enjoyed most about her new job, having Gillian and Cliff Gallup as neighbors was near the top of the list. Port Ainslie was pretty, and her lakeside cottage at Willow Cove was lovely. Geegee and Cliff's friendship and generous nature made it all much better.

When Max arrived home that evening, Geegee had flagged her down. *Got a fire in the fireplace and a kettle on the stove*, she had called out to Max. *And shortbread in the oven. How's that sound?*

Sound's like I'll be there in five minutes, Max had said. And now here she was, seated by the fire with a good friend. Some people, Max knew, needed drugs to relax. Having a neighbor like Geegee was much better.

"Cliff has classes to teach." Geegee looked at her watch. "Won't be home until after nine. You eaten yet?"

Max shook her head. The tea, the pastry and the company were warm on a cold night. But she still had a murder to solve. On her own, if she could. "Sorry," she said. "Can't stay for dinner."

"Listen, kiddo," Geegee said, "you have to eat and take care of yourself. I can whip up…"

Max cut her off. "What do you know about painting?" she said.

Geegee folded her arms and leaned against the kitchen table. "You got a color picked out for your cupboards? I told you we can get it done…"

Max waved her words away. "Not that kind of painting. Didn't you say you studied art when you went to college in Toronto?"

Geegee frowned. "Max," she said, her voice lower. "We're painting cupboards, right? We're not painting another *Mona Lisa*. All we need is paint, a couple of brushes, some masking tape and a bottle of pinot grigio."

"This isn't about the cupboards. This is about the body we found on Bridge Road this morning."

By noon the entire town had learned that Robert Morton's body had been found on Bridge Road. Most people knew he was naked. Some had heard that the corpse was frozen as well. Geegee, Max knew, was eager to hear details but did not dare ask. *Sorry*, Max had said the first time Geegee raised a question about some crime in town. *I can't talk about police matters.*

I understand, Geegee had said. She tried to hide her disappointment with a smile. *But we're still friends, right?*

Now Max was ready to talk to her about the frozen and naked body. "Maybe you can help me," she said. "With this murder."

Geegee almost ran to sit next to Max. She rested a hand on Max's arm. "Ask me anything," she said. She sounded as though she were running out of breath. "Was he a painter, this Morton guy? An artist? I think I know the house. Big place on the hill. But he worked at a new-car place, right? Or was *she* a painter, his wife? She's a snob, I know that." When Max said nothing, Geegee sat back and said, more slowly, "So what do you want to know?"

"Did you visit any art galleries for your painting classes?" Max said.

Geegee frowned. "Some. This was, you know, nearly twenty years ago. But we went out to a few galleries to look at their stuff, sometimes talk to the owners."

"Do you know one called the Elendt Gallery?"

"It's not *Ee*-lent," Geegee said. "You say it as *El*-ent. It's German. The gallery has been around for years."

"What do you know about it?"

"Small place. No big names. No Group of Seven painters, anything like that. Just good local artists. The couple that owns it, or used to, they knew their stuff. But like I say, that was a lot of years ago. I don't know if it's still in business."

"It is," Max said. "I checked. I think I'll go there tomorrow."

"Not," Geegee said, "to buy some art."

"No," Max said. "To find some answers."

"Promise you'll tell me what you can when you get back."

"It'll cost you another piece of shortbread."

Geegee almost jumped to her feet. "Take the whole damn pan!" she said.

SIX

"I don't mean to second-guess you," Margie said, "but aren't you supposed to share data with the OPP?"

It was the next morning. The day had dawned just as frigid as all the other days, but more gloomy and overcast.

"Please don't lecture me, Margie," Max said. She buttoned her tunic, reached for the keys to her police car and glanced at the clock. "If all goes well, I should get there before noon. Could be back here by three or before. You or Henry call me about anything I need to know. If anyone asks, I am fulfilling my duties as police chief."

"In Toronto?" Margie said as Max walked out the door. "On Bloor Street?" she added as the door closed.

———

Max loved driving a marked police car on the highway. She would stay within the 100-kilometers-per-hour speed limit at first and watch other drivers slow their pace to match hers. The OPP gave tickets or a warning only if drivers were going more than 120 kilometers per hour. Still, no one wanted to pass a police car moving at the limit. On the way to Toronto she kept her speed at exactly 100. Then, after leading cars in a law-abiding parade for about 10 kilometers, she increased her speed to 120. When she did, and all the drivers around her sped up to match that, she could almost feel their relief.

She had left Muskoka on a cold, gray day. But halfway to Toronto the sky opened to a rich blue. The sun shone brightly, and when Max lowered the window and stuck her hand into the air, it felt lovely and warm. Now that's just not fair, she thought. The big city gets July, and we get winter. She told herself the warm air would soon be on its way north to Port Ainslie. But somehow she doubted it.

———

Elendt Gallery was in Bloor West Village, a high-class part of town. Several works of art hung in the display window. The gallery name and hours were written in gold lettering on the window glass.

Looking through the glass door, Max saw white walls and gray carpet. She had not been inside many galleries, but this looked familiar to her. Everything, she realized, was chosen to show off the paintings well.

She stepped inside. The tinkle of a small bell sounded as the door closed behind her. She stopped and looked around.

Soft music played from hidden speakers. Paintings hung on all the walls. Through an open door at the rear, Max could see into a small office. A woman in a turtleneck and skirt sat in front of a computer.

Max walked through the room, looking at the art. Some paintings were done by the same artist whose work Max had seen in Beth Morton's home.

When the woman in the office looked up to see Max in her police uniform, the smile she'd put on faded. She rose from the chair and said, "Can I help you?" Her voice was rich and warm.

"I'm looking for a man named Steve Carson," Max said. "Would you know where I could reach him?"

"Stevie?" the woman said. "He's not here anymore. Hasn't been for quite a while.

Why are you looking for him?" The woman was taller than Max.

"You say he's no longer here," Max said. "Did he work here?"

"Yes. Yes, he did," the woman said.

"Have you seen him lately?"

"No, not for some time."

"But he did work here."

"Yes, he did."

"And you sold his art here."

"We still do. Older works." She nodded to some paintings by Carson.

"May I ask your name, please?"

"It's Sandra. May I ask why you're looking for him?"

"It's a police matter." Max took out her notebook and began writing. "When did you see him last?"

"About four and a half years ago. No one has seen him since."

"No one?"

Sandra shook her head.

"I was told he was in Muskoka last week," Max said.

"Is that right?" She looked surprised.

"He's a bit of a rover, I heard," Max said. "But a very good painter."

"One of the most talented I know."

"Do you have any idea where I could find him?"

"If he was seen in Muskoka, I suggest you start there." Sandra seemed edgy.

"If he travels a lot," Max said, "I guess he could be anywhere." She wanted to keep this woman talking.

"I guess so." Sandra spread her hands. "If there's anything else I can do for you…" She tilted her head toward the office. "I have some work to finish."

Did I drive all this way for nothing? Max asked herself. She had looked for answers. All she'd gotten were more questions. Where had this guy Steve been for the last four and a half years? Why had he shown up just before his sister's husband was found dead and frozen in a ditch? What about the black pickup truck? Who was driving it? If he wasn't Beth's brother, who was he? Max was sure Beth had lied to her about her brother. But she couldn't add up all the lies she thought she had heard.

"I may stay for a moment and admire the artwork," Max said. "I like some of the paintings. Might buy one for my home, if I can afford it."

Sandra's smile said she didn't think Max could afford more than an empty frame. "Let me know if I can help you," she said as she walked back to her office.

Max saw three paintings similar to the one in Beth's home. They were not as large, and they were not as abstract either. In one, Max could make out a stream that flowed through a dark green forest. Another had waves crashing on bare rocks. The third held Max's gaze. If she stood back and closed her eyes a little, she could see wild-flowers in a crystal vase.

Whoever painted them, Max decided, had known Stephen Carson's work and tried to copy it. Max knew enough about art to figure that out. But this artist had added more realism, which Max liked. The work lacked the angry tone she had seen in the painting in Beth Morton's home. She imagined this painting of flowers hanging in her own living room. It appealed to her. She had always thought about collecting art. Maybe this was the time and place to start.

She lifted a corner of the painting away from the wall. On the back was the same Elendt Gallery label she had seen in Beth's home. That painting, however, had not had a price on it. This one did. Ten thousand dollars.

The frame made a soft *thunk* as Max let it swing back against the wall.

"Is everything all right?"

Max turned to see Sandra leaning back from her chair to look into the gallery area.

"Everything's fine."

Sandra kept watching her.

"Actually, I think I have all I need," Max said. She waved a hand. "Thanks for your help."

Sandra turned back to her computer screen.

Max thought, Must be nice to be able to buy paintings like these. She looked for the first time at the artist's signature in the bottom right-hand corner. *Wait a minute.* She looked again at the artist's name on the label, then from the painting to the office. All she could see was the woman's back. The rest of her and the computer were hidden.

Max recalled the view when she arrived of Sandra walking toward her in slim skirt and turtleneck top. She moved to one side of the room so Sandra could not see her.

Then she walked lightly toward the office and stepped in front of the open door.

Not loudly but urgently, Max said, "Stephen! Stephen Carson!"

The woman started and turned to face Max, her mouth slightly open. She had responded, Max knew, to the name that had once been hers.

SEVEN

"**B**eth was always ashamed of me," Sandra Carson said. They were in the office, she and Max, seated on metal chairs. A coffeemaker sighed in the corner.

Max had told her why she was there. She said that Bob Morton had been found murdered. That's when Sandra invited Max to have coffee with her in the office. Sandra needed to talk. "I learned not to trust police over the years," she said. "They called me and people like me the usual names. And I tend to protect myself from strangers. Where Beth is involved..." She shrugged. Then she told Max her story in soft, flat tones.

She had spent much of her life feeling like a woman trapped in a man's body. As a teenager she had told her parents and sister about it, wanting their love and support. *I am not a boy*, she said to them. She had tapped her chest with her hand. *Not in here. Not in my heart*. Her parents tried to take the news as best they could, and she loved them for that.

"But Beth never got over it," she said. "She told me I had shamed her and our family. I had not shamed anyone. She was just afraid the people she tried to impress would think less of her. They would judge her for having a brother who wanted to be her sister."

Sandra poured herself a cup of coffee. She held the pot toward Max, who shook her head.

"I grew angry at her...and at myself and the world for what and who I was," she said. "I poured all of that anger into my art. It's not there now, the anger. And my art has changed."

She told Max she had been running the gallery for five years. The owners lived in New York City. "They sell my work in New York," she said. "They leave me to run things here. As long as I make money here and my work still sells in New York, I am on my own."

"Sounds like a good deal," Max said.

"It is. But it can get lonely. Not many people come to galleries anymore. They buy on the Internet." She smiled. "I welcome the chance to have a chat, even with a police officer." Then the smile was gone. "Too bad it involves my sister."

"So you are still upset about the way she treated you?" Max asked.

"That and other stuff."

Max wondered what *other stuff* meant, but she said nothing.

"She never wanted me around," Sandra said. "Even when my work brought good reviews and prices, she wanted nothing to do with me. She wouldn't come to see my work or talk about it. She did not even tell me about her marriage to Frank Higgs. I was never invited to her la-de-da dinner parties. She would have other artists, but never me. And when Mom and Dad died just six weeks apart, she didn't let me know. I was in Paris at the time. She knew where I was and how to reach me, but she didn't…"

Her voice broke, and she lowered her head. She covered her eyes with her hand. "She buried them and never said a word to me. I wrote her to ask why Mom and Dad didn't answer my letters. There was never a reply. I had to come home to learn…"

Max reached out to touch Sandra's shoulder.

Sandra sat up and smiled. "I'm all right," she said. "Thank you." She dabbed at her eyes with a tissue.

Max said, "I saw one of your paintings in Beth's living room. So she must like your work."

"No, she doesn't," Sandra said. "When I was going through the change from male to female…" She stopped. Then: "It was… it cost a lot of money. More than I had. Thousands of dollars more. I went to her and Frank to ask for help. I promised to pay them back when I was able to paint again. It was so important to me."

Beth, Sandra said, would not even talk about it. "She made me feel so small." But Beth's husband agreed to help. "Frank Higgs was a sweet, classy man. I adored him, which upset Beth. He came to the gallery, liked that painting and gave me ten thousand dollars for it. I accepted, of course. Beth was furious, but Frank insisted. Frank…" Her eyes grew wet again, and she lowered her head.

"What is it?" Max asked.

"Never mind."

Sandra sat upright and began again. She said she'd always wanted to be close to her sister. Beth had rejected her as Stephen and still did, now that she was Sandra. She knew how much Beth disliked her brother's need to change gender. Sandra had even promised that she would erase every trace of Stephen Carson. *You will never have had a brother*, she said to Beth. *The world will never know. You will not be embarrassed anymore.*

Sandra shook her head. "I told her that over and over. It was the only way Beth would even agree that I existed. I tried so hard to destroy proof that there was once a man named Stephen Carson. About the only things left are my birth record and the paintings I signed as Stephen. But she still will have nothing to do with me."

"Now you sign them as Sandra Carson," Max said. "That's what gave me the clue out there." She pointed to the gallery. "Along with your voice."

"Which is deep," Sandra said.

"Not too deep."

"And my hands. They're big. I hate them. And my turtleneck. I wear high collars all the time. Even in summer. They were not able to remove my Adam's apple, so I hide it." Sandra smiled. "You know, all those feminists are right...it's not easy being a woman."

Max needed to get back on track. "Beth said you were the young man who stayed at her house the week before her husband left. She told me knowing that Stephen Carson could not be traced."

"Not easily. Anyway, it was not me. Not a chance."

"Who do you think this young man was?"

"I think he may have a number, not a name."

"What do you mean?"

"My sister has a thing for young men. Always has. What did they use to call women her age that acted like that? Cougars? Well, Beth is a first-class cougar. Of course, up in Port Ainslie the kind of young men Beth likes are not as easy to pick up as they are here."

"Why is she living there?"

"It's where Frank wanted to live. It was his money, after all. Beth would rather have stayed here in the city. When she saw the house that Frank wanted to buy, she changed her mind. She loved it. Loved it much more than she loved Frank." Sandra shrugged. "Beth got the house when Frank died. She got everything when Frank died. She also got Bob, who left his wife and kids for her."

"What was Bob like?"

"Good-looking man. Five or six years younger than Beth."

"Was he a heavy drinker?"

"If he was, I think Beth drove him to it."

"How well did you know Bob?"

"I met him twice. I went north in the fall last year to get some ideas for painting." She waved a hand toward the gallery. "One of them is out there. I took a room at a B&B and went to visit Beth. I had this crazy idea that we might be able to get along as sisters. Bob answered the door and said Beth didn't want to see me. When he said I should go away, I was crushed all over again. I think Bob felt sorry for me. He learned where I was staying and invited me to meet him the next day. At the place where he worked. So I went. I thought he was a nice man, but a sad one. He still felt guilty about leaving his family for Beth. I think he believed he'd made a big mistake. Beth drank too much, and Bob was sure she cheated on him. And she scared him."

"How?"

"She could be violent. She would throw things at him. Dishes. Books. Knives."

"Did he say anything that might link your sister to his murder?"

Sandra thought for a moment. "I don't know," she said finally.

"You don't know, or you can't say?"

"I just don't know. Only that Bob had reason to be scared of her."

Max could see Beth Morton as a mean drunk. It seemed to fit. She had learned quite a bit about the woman. She wasn't sure what it all meant or if it would help her solve the murder of Bob Morton. But she knew she would have a lot to think about during her drive back to Port Ainslie.

She stood, thanked Sandra Carson for her time and said she was sorry if she had upset Sandra with her questions.

"The most upsetting part," Sandra said, "was talking about Frank Higgs."

"You must have liked him a lot," Max said.

Sandra nodded. "Did you hear how he died?"

"Drowned in their swimming pool."

"That's one story."

Max stopped, her hand on the door to Bloor Street. "What's the other?"

When Sandra told her, Max knew she had more to think about on the way back to Port Ainslie. Far more than she had expected.

EIGHT

"She murdered her first husband."

Max was back in her office in Port Ainslie. It was almost three o'clock. The sky was as gray and the air as chilly as when she left that morning. Margie sat across from her. Henry leaned against the wall, listening, his arms folded.

"Bob Morton told Sandra about it when Sandra, who used to be Beth's brother, visited last year," Max said. She had described the first part of her interview with Sandra Carson. Now she was revealing the rest of what Sandra had told her.

"Frank Higgs, Beth's first husband, had a serious heart problem. He needed medication three times a day." Max looked from Margie to Henry and back again as she spoke. "One night when Beth was drunk and angry with Bob, her second husband, she said nobody except her knew what happened to Frank. And she told him. She bragged about it. Or maybe she thought it would scare Bob. I'm sure it did."

Beth said she had replaced Higgs's heart pills with sugar pills for a week. When he began to complain about chest pains, she said he needed to relax with a swim in the pool. Once he was in the water, she began pushing him under with a long pole used to clean the pool.

"He must have known what she was doing," Max said. "And he was already in pain. He had a massive heart attack, there in the pool. Just like Beth planned. She told the police she tried to rescue him, but he couldn't grip the pole. Nobody thought about it. The coroner confirmed a heart attack, and she had the body cremated the next day."

"Why wouldn't he come to us?" Henry said. "The second husband? Why wouldn't he tell us what he knew?"

"What proof would he have?" Max said. "All he could tell us is what he told Sandra. Beth would deny it, of course. The whole thing would be useless in court. You can't get a murder conviction on that kind of tale. What we need to do now is get her for the murder of Bob, her second husband."

"What about the young man she picked up?" Margie said. "The one she said was her brother? He had to be in on it."

"Find him and you might solve the case," Henry added.

"The question is," Max said, "do we tell Beth Morton that we know she lied to us about him being her brother? Or do we stay quiet and try to catch her in a bigger lie?"

"We?" Margie said. "There's that matter of sharing what we know with the OPP. If they find that you tried to hide evidence from them…"

"I know, I know." Max held her head in her hands. "I'll call Boucher tomorrow. I'll tell him what I know and ask if he needs a report from me." She looked from Margie to Henry. "I hate to do it. I told Sandra I would protect her privacy as much as I could. When the OPP hears about her, they'll rush a team to Toronto and spread her name in all the papers."

"Maybe you don't have to talk about her," Margie said. "Unless they order you to."

———

"You didn't give me squat," Boucher said when Max called the next morning. Max had told him Beth Morton did not have a brother. She said she had learned this by speaking to someone in Toronto.

"Actually, she does have a brother. This was in my report, in case you failed to read it. We knew that from our computer files," he said. "By going all the way to Toronto, you went beyond your bounds. You just wasted time and gasoline. It took you all day to find out what we were able to learn in seconds. That's why you people up there should stop playing detective. From now on, leave the serious stuff to us."

Max had not had time to say that Beth once had a brother who was now her sister. Just that she did not have a brother. Hearing Boucher's words, she chose not to pass on the news about Sandra Carson to him now. Maybe later. Maybe never. "If you knew she had lied to us about her brother," she said, "why didn't you tell us? Aren't we all to share what we know?"

"No, Chief Benson," Boucher said. He spat the word *Chief* as if it were a joke. "This is not a two-way street. You share all you know with us. We do not need to share what we know with you. And we won't."

"Why not?"

"Because we figure any secret stuff we might pass on to you will not stay secret. If you get my drift."

"I don't get your drift. Talk in plain words, please."

"I just did. Anything else I can do for you?"

"Did you speak to Beth Morton about her lie? Can you tell me that?"

"Yes, we did, since you asked. She claims her brother is mentally ill. He's a nutcase who spends his life erasing all records of his life. So as far as she is concerned, she does not have a brother."

"Do you believe it?"

"Could be true."

"Where are we with the investigation?"

"If by *we* you mean the OPP, we are checking trucks that match the one driven by the man Beth Morton says is her brother."

"A black Ford F-150."

"Correct."

"How many are there in the country?"

"Thousands. Tens of thousands."

"Then you are looking for the wrong thing."

"What does that mean?" Boucher said.

Max had hung up.

———

Max spent the rest of the day drinking too much coffee and reading the OPP report too many times. By noon she was confused and angry. Confused by the facts she had that might let her arrest Beth Morton, and angry over the insults from Boucher.

She understood his need to keep things under wraps, but she had done nothing to suggest he couldn't trust her. She had respect for the OPP and its people. That wasn't the point. She just wanted them to accept that she could solve a major crime like murder. Or at least be an asset to them. Didn't her twenty years as a cop in Toronto count?

Many crimes, she knew, were solved by hard-working cops searching for links between people, places and events. The best way to solve a murder case was to study the facts. You looked for facts that matched. When they didn't match, you went looking for reasons to explain things. She was sure that was how the murder of Bob Morton would be solved. Find the claims that were true, and follow the ones that were false.

"The phone hasn't rung all morning," Margie said at noon. She had brought a bowl of homemade chicken soup and a square of corn bread for her lunch. She was about to put it all in the microwave oven. "I can't believe I'm having chicken soup and corn bread for lunch in June," she said. "I should be eating salad and cold poached salmon." She looked over at Max. "Want to share this with me?"

"Thanks, but I'll drive home and eat there," Max said. She reached for the keys to her cruiser. "It'll give me a chance to think."

Max did not go home for lunch. Instead, she drove to Sunset Hill.

Beth Morton answered Max's knock. She opened her front door just wide enough to look out. Her eyes flew from Max to the cruiser and back.

"I wonder if I can speak to you," Max said.

"About what?" Beth lifted her chin and glared at Max.

"About the death of your husband."

"I've been told not to talk to you."

"By whom?"

"By the OPP. I am to talk only with Constable Boucher or his staff. Not you."

"I just need to ask…"

The door closed.

Max had wanted to see how Beth would react to the news that Max had met Sandra Carson. They would have much to talk about, she was sure…if she could get Beth to discuss it. The more suspects talk, Max knew, the more likely they are to say something they didn't mean to say. That's what she had hoped would happen in a visit with Beth. Now it seemed like another of her ideas that had gone nowhere.

Maybe, Max thought as she drove down Sunset Hill, she should let Boucher and his pros do whatever they wanted to do. She, Margie and Henry could sit and wait for summer to arrive. They could relax like tourists.

She called Margie from the car and asked if anything was new. Margie said no calls had come in. The cool and overcast weather just might be making people obey the law more than normal. Maybe we shouldn't hope for warm weather after all, Max thought. She told Margie to call her at home if she was needed. Then she drove to Willow Cove, made herself lunch and ate in her kitchen looking over the lake. She would have liked to sit on her porch in warm sunshine, but it was still too cold and gloomy.

She was about to return to the police station when Geegee appeared at the kitchen window, a plate of shortbread in her hand. The smile on her face and her raised eyebrows made Max laugh out loud.

"I'm here to trade for dirt," Geegee said when Max opened the door. "What can you tell me about that body you found the other day?"

"Nothing," Max said, setting the shortbread on the table and reaching for the coffee pot. "Not yet. You take cream, right?"

"Black." Geegee looked hurt. "Boy, I thought living next to the chief of police would liven up my dull life a little."

"Sorry," Max said. "Tell you what." She picked up her cell phone. "You can listen in while I get all the news from Action Central. How's that?"

"Action Central?" Geegee said. "In cold Port Ainslie? What, you're gonna call Tim Hortons?"

Max had already dialed Margie. "I may take another hour here for lunch," she said when Margie answered. "Any reason to come in?" She switched the phone to speaker mode, ready to make notes if needed.

"Only to send some stuff to Boucher like you promised," Margie said.

"I'll draft it when I come in later. Where's Henry?"

"Out on patrol. He likes to crank up the heat in the car higher than here. He says I don't feel the cold as much as him 'cause I'm still getting hot flashes. I told him that was sexist, and he said, *What isn't these days?* I was glad to see the back of him."

"What's happened since I left this morning?"

"Got a note that the old cruiser's due for an oil change next week," Margie said. "Those folks on Creek Road said not to worry about that generator that was stolen last week 'cause it's back. Carter's dog was out with no leash again. Henry picked up the dog and warned them. Again. Expect another box of candy. Town council wants a budget review next month. Plus you missed some good soup. I'll bring you a bowl tomorrow."

"I'll be back by two," Max said. "See you then." She switched off the phone and looked at Geegee. "So there you are," she said. "How's that for true crime in Port Ainslie? You're not going to hear that kind of news out of Hollywood, are you?" She reached for a piece of shortbread.

"Kind of strange, isn't it?" Geegee was resting her chin on her hand.

"Not strange. Perfectly normal week around here."

"I mean the generator thing. People report it's stolen. Then they say it's back. Like somebody borrowed it. Whoever took it in the first place."

"Well, maybe they…," Max began.

"Like, if you steal something from somebody, why would you take it back? You'd be as likely to get caught putting it back as you would stealing it, right? So why'd they do it? Did they feel guilty or something?"

Max sat frozen, listening.

"And taking it back doesn't mean there was no crime. If you take ten bucks out of my purse and put it back later, you're still a thief, right? So why didn't these people want you to do something about it?"

Max almost jumped out of her chair.

"Where're you going?" Geegee said.

"I'm not sure," Max said. She was slipping one arm into her tunic. In her free hand she was calling Margie on her cell phone. "Margie," Geegee heard her say as she went out the door, "tell me about that stolen generator."

NINE

Port Ainslie's town limits stretched along the shore of the lake and up the face of Granite Mountain. The boundary covered a lot of land. Yet the town could afford only a chief, a constable, Margie Burns and two cars.

There were few crimes to solve in Port Ainslie. Residents just didn't seem interested in breaking the law. Not much of it anyway. Port Ainslie had a lot of land, but it had few criminals. Still, the townspeople liked the idea of having their own police force, small as it was. *Waste of money*, some folks said, meaning the police budget.

Stubborn fools, the OPP called the town and its council. It didn't matter. The people in Port Ainslie were more independent than others in Muskoka. They wanted to police themselves, without outsiders. Including the OPP. They took pride in being the only town of its size to have its own police force. Such as it was.

When people pointed out that Port Ainslie was not like other towns in the area, they meant its refusal to be patrolled by the OPP.

They might also have meant the way it was split in two by Ainslie Creek.

Most people lived...or wanted to live... in West Ainslie. It had the best beaches, and included Sunset Hill and Willow Cove. East Ainslie was rocky and raw, with forest and brush but few homes. This led to people saying they lived either "across the creek" or "up the creek." Living up the creek meant in East Ainslie.

The people who had reported the generator stolen, then returned, were Jack and Flo Brenner. They lived on Creek Road, the dividing line between East and West Ainslie. They had told Margie they wanted to forget about the theft of the generator. Why? Because it had been brought back. They were fine with that. But where had it been for more than a week? They didn't know. And why didn't they want the thief caught? They didn't say.

Many people in Muskoka kept portable generators to be used when the electric power failed. This could happen in midwinter. Heavy snows could break the power lines and it could take days to restore the electricity. When the temperature reaches 25 or 30 below in Muskoka and furnaces don't run, you need a large wood stove. Or a generator.

This spring had been cold, yet not so cold that anyone would need a portable generator. But someone needed it for a week and then didn't need it again. They needed the power badly enough to steal a generator. Then they brought it back. On one level this didn't make sense. On another level it made perfect sense.

She had no problem finding the Brenner home. A painted sign said *Jack & Flo's Creek Side Nest* above a drawing of two rocking chairs. The sign would have been too cute for words in the big city. On Creek Road in Port Ainslie, it looked right at home.

———

"We are sorry if we caused trouble," Flo Brenner said. She handed Max a cup of coffee and pushed some butter tarts toward her. She was in her fifties, not as old as Max had expected.

"Just did what we should have done," Jack Brenner said. He leaned against the sink, a tall man with white hair and a warm smile. "Didn't know who took it, did we? Only use it when the power's out. That was...how often last year, Flo?"

"Twice, I think," his wife said. "We ran it after that ice storm last March. We had lights, television and the fridge all week long till the power came back. More than most people had. People with furnaces, like our neighbors, they near froze to death."

"Where do you store your generator?" Max asked.

"In the garage." Jack Brenner looked away.

"Do you think someone knew it was there?"

"I guess so."

"Why did they bring the generator back?"

No one spoke. Max kept looking at Jack, who looked at Flo. Flo looked out the window at the garden. Max sipped her coffee, watching them both. Then: "Who brought it back?"

Jack said, "Our nephew."

Max turned to Flo, still looking at the garden. "His name is Ted," Flo said. "Ted Huffman."

"Don't need more trouble," Jack said. "Ted don't."

"So he took the generator," Max said, "and didn't tell you about it. Then he brought it back."

"And said he was sorry." Jack pushed away from the sink to stand near his wife. "He's family. You tend to forgive family."

"He's my sister's boy," Flo said. "She and her husband moved to BC ten years ago."

"They ran a maple camp here," Jack said. "Back in the bush, near the falls. That's where they boiled down sap and made syrup, all that stuff. They sold the land to some outfit, said they would build houses on it. Never did a thing. Land's sat there since. Outfit says they want to sell it if they can make enough profit from it.

It's all about money these days." He made a face.

"He went with them for a while to BC," Flo said. "Ted did."

"Got into some trouble out there. Kind of a wild kid, he is," Jack said. "Still call him a kid. He's a man now."

"What kind of trouble?" Max said.

"Usual kind, a young man like that," Flo said. "He likes the girls, and the girls like him. Loves to have his fun."

"Did a few months in jail for theft," Jack said.

Flo made a face at her husband's words.

"Sorry," Jack said. "But it's true. The police here, they could find out anyway." He looked at Max. "Isn't that right?"

"Tell me about Ted," Max said. "When have you seen him over the past two weeks?"

Flo told Max that Ted had shown up to ask if he could stay with them for a while. "Came by sometime last month," she said.

"Didn't call ahead to ask if he could stay. Just pulled in the driveway with a smile and a hug. And a suitcase."

"Showed up with a handful of *Gimme* and a mouthful of *Much obliged*," Jack said.

"Told us he was on his way east to look for work on an offshore oil rig," Flo said. "He's not a bad boy. Just a little wild. We remember him as a youngster."

"Took him fishing," Jack said. He turned to stare out the window. "Taught him that. Taught him a few things when he was a good little guy."

The first week went well, they told Max. Ted slept in a spare bedroom, helped with some chores, kept to himself.

"Then one night he came home and he'd been drinking," Flo said. "Been drinking a lot. Could hardly stand up."

"Told him we didn't want him drinking," Jack said. "He wanted to drink, he'd have to go elsewhere. He didn't listen."

"Two nights later he's just as drunk, but this time he has a woman with him," Flo said.

"She was as drunk as he was," Jack said. "Some tramp."

"We told him to find another place to stay," Flo said.

"He laughed and said okay, but not until the morning." Jack shook his head from side to side. "Had to put up with the sound of them giggling and groaning all night long."

"They left at dawn," Flo said. Her expression changed to sadness. "I was glad to see him go, but sorry too. Like I said, he's not really a bad..."

Jack interrupted his wife. "We thought he would head for Toronto. Or Nova Scotia. But he stayed around these parts. Saw him downtown once or twice. Then we didn't see him until he came here the day before yesterday. He brought our generator back. Said he was sorry he took it."

"Asked us not to tell the police," Flo said. "But we thought we should tell you not to keep looking for it."

"Where had he been living?" Max said.

"Don't know," Jack said. "But he didn't look too good."

Max asked what he meant.

"Kind of scruffy."

"He was dressed well when we saw him downtown a few times," Flo said. "Had some new clothes. Got a haircut."

"Didn't look too good yesterday," Jack said. "Hadn't shaved for a while. Lost a bit of weight too."

Max finished her coffee. "Where can I find him now?"

"No idea," Jack said.

"Don't have a clue," Flo said.

"How did he get around?" Max said. "He didn't walk everywhere. You said he pulled into your driveway one night. In what?"

"A truck," Flo said. "He drove it all the way from BC."

Max felt her pulse quicken. "What kind of truck?"

"Pickup," Jack said. "Black Ford."

"Thank you," Max said. She forced herself not to leap out of the chair and run for her car. She was doing police work, but that didn't mean she had to be rude. "By the way, do you own a freezer? A full-size model?"

Both shook their heads.

Max thanked them for their help and said she needed to leave right away.

"Take a tart with you," Flo said and handed her one.

On the way to the front door, Max turned and said, "Where did you say that sugar camp is?"

TEN

The area around Ainslie Falls is wooded with maple trees. Some had been damaged in a late-spring ice storm. Broken limbs covered much of the ground. A few trees had died. Some had only a few leaves.

Max drove slowly along the road, looking for a lane into the woods. She found one and saw that someone had cleared the road of broken branches. But there were too many to believe they had all fallen from trees. The large ones had been used to block the path into the woods.

She recalled her parents taking her to a maple-syrup camp. She had been a child, maybe six years old. The memory was still clear to her. There had been wood fires under metal vats filled with boiling sap. Horse-drawn sleds came from deep in the woods, carrying barrels of sap. She watched the clear sap being poured into the vats. She could still taste the hot syrup that had been spread on the snow to harden into toffee. The visit taught her about life in the bush and how much goodness could come from trees and nature.

All of this came back to her as she drove deeper into the shadow of the woods. She was glad she had called Margie to say where she was. Margie had asked… no, demanded…*What in the blazes are you doing out there all alone?* Max said she would explain later.

Margie had been right to ask. The deeper Max drove into the woods, the darker it became.

After a kilometer or so the road curved and rose ahead of her. At the top of the rise she saw a large wooden building to the left. It was badly in need of repair and a coat of fresh paint. A pickup truck coated with mud was parked nearby. It was a black Ford with BC license plates.

Max parked the cruiser and stepped out, her gun in her hand. She looked into the truck's cab, then turned to the building and called out, "Is anybody here?" Hearing no answer, she walked to the door and looked inside.

The building was empty. Well, almost empty.

From the doorway Max could see a large sleeping bag on the wooden floor. A pair of torn jeans, two T-shirts, a jacket and worn boots lay nearby. Old potato-chip bags, soft-drink cans and coffee cups were everywhere.

She stepped inside. A large cardboard box sat on a low table in the corner. She walked to it and looked inside. Dishes, knives and forks sat among salt and pepper shakers, cooking oil, a cast-iron pan and a large knife. Next to the box was a camp stove. Someone had made their home here for a week or more.

Max walked to a window on the far side of the building, looked out and caught her breath. There it was. A large white box with a hinged cover and a black power cord. The kind of home freezer a family would use to store food. Or something else.

Had she the time, Max might have felt smug. But she had no time. A glimpse of movement on the path to the creek caught her eye. She hurried to the other window and stood to one side, looking down the path.

The young man walking toward her carried a fishing rod over one shoulder. His other hand held a rope strung through the mouths and gills of two large trout.

He did not look pleased about his catch. He looked nervous and frightened. One moment he seemed to fear someone would leap from the bushes. The next moment he appeared as though he might break down and cry. He also looked sad and lonely. Almost in spite of herself, Max felt a pang of sadness for him. He was a handsome young man who would grow into a handsome adult someday. As he drew closer Max could see the blue in his eyes, the curl in his fair hair and the lean frame. He knows what he has done, she thought. He just doesn't know how soon it will all be over. What a waste of a life.

Coming from the creek, the young man couldn't see Max's car parked behind the old building. At the open door he set his rod against the wall and walked inside. His mind appeared to be elsewhere, perhaps thinking about the trout he would fry for his dinner.

He looked up to see Max. The sight of her appeared to shock him as much as the sight of the gun in her hand. "Ted Huffman," she said, "I am arresting you for the murder of Robert Morton."

Huffman stared back at her. He chose not to speak and didn't move. His shoulders sagged, and he looked down at his feet.

"Turn around and place your hands behind your back," Max said, her gun aimed at his chest. "Keep your wrists together." Max pulled the handcuffs from her belt. "If you try to flee, I will use my weapon. I will aim for your legs, but I could hit you anywhere. So do what I say."

Huffman did a strange thing. He smiled. Then he dropped the fish and turned his back to her, his wrists together. "Believe it or not," he said, "I'm glad to see you. I'm glad it's over."

Max put the cuffs on his wrists. Then she warned him that anything he said could be used against him. If he could not afford a lawyer, one would be provided. The usual stuff.

With her free hand on his elbow, she marched Huffman to her cruiser. Outside the building, he looked this way and that, as though searching for someone. "It's just you?" he said when she opened the rear door of the car. "There's nobody else here? You did this all by yourself?"

"All by myself," she said. She placed a hand on his head to push him down and into the cruiser.

"You must be one hell of a cop," he said.

"Actually, I'm the chief," Max said and closed the door. Slipping behind the wheel, she saw the butter tart she had set on the dashboard after leaving the Brenner home. She reached for it and then looked in the rear view mirror at Huffman. "I'd share this with you," she said, "but I think I earned it." When he said nothing she added, "Too bad those nice trout you caught will go to waste."

The paved road back to the highway seemed shorter this time. Seeing it ahead, Max called Margie. "Get a holding cell ready," she said. "Then call those guys in Cranston. Tell them I've arrested the prime suspect in the murder of Bob Morton."

Margie hooted with joy through the police radio. She called out to Henry in the station, "She got him! She got the killer!"

Max tried to tell Margie to calm down, but Henry's voice over the radio interrupted her. He asked if it was true and how Max had done it and what the guy looked like. Max cut him off and told him and Margie to act like professionals. "This is not a joke," she said. "A young man is facing a charge of murder. We have to respect the law and all that it means."

Margie and Henry went silent, and Max felt guilty about her speech. "But I know what you mean," she said. "We proved something to a lot of people. We proved we can do all the things they expect of us. And we will. But let's save the party for later, all right?"

She was so busy lecturing that she failed to see the silver Mercedes-Benz speeding away toward Sunset Hill.

ELEVEN

"I'll say one thing for him," Margie said.

She had just come back into the office after serving Huffman sandwiches and coffee. She'd put him in the cell with a view of the parking lot. "He's one good-looking young man." She glanced out the window. "Here comes another one."

Max looked up from her notes to see Ronald Boucher stepping out of his OPP car. "This one," she said, "might give me more trouble than the guy we just locked up."

When Boucher entered the station he treated Max and Margie as though they were blocking traffic on a busy street. "I'm here for the prisoner," he said.

No hello and no smile. "Give me what I need to sign, and I'm on my way."

"What we will give you," Max said, "is a chance to sit in the room with me. While I question him."

"We will do that in Cranston," Boucher said. "And we will record his statement. On video. With three cameras." He looked around the station. "Do you have the means to do that?"

"No," Max said. "We have an old Sony tape recorder that still works. And a nice room with three chairs and a picture of the Queen. More than that, we have the legal right to talk to him first because the crime took place here in our town."

Boucher rolled his eyes.

"There's more," Max said. "Margie has the key to his cell. She will not use it to let Huffman out until I ask her to."

Boucher turned to see Margie holding a large metal ring. Two keys hung from it.

He looked back at Max and said, "You're cute, you know that?" His sarcasm hung in the air like a bad odor.

"No, I'm not," Max said. "I'm a small-town cop who wants to see things done the way they're supposed to be done. I will not do things the way somebody else wants me to do them. Unless I agree. And right now I don't." She took the keys from Margie and began to walk to the cells. "Let's get started."

Ted Huffman proved more than willing to talk. He answered each question Max asked him. He was polite and sometimes seemed about to cry.

As the young man spoke, Max looked at him more closely. Margie was right. This was a handsome guy with a lean and strong body. He was also, Max felt, not the type of young man to commit murder.

Raise a little hell now and then, sure. And break a lot of young girls' hearts, without a doubt.

The country was full of men like him... young, good-looking guys who liked girls, pickup trucks, beer and hockey. By age thirty most would be married with kids, a job and memories. Those young men were many things. But most were not murderers.

Max knew Ted Huffman had killed Bob Morton. But from the moment she saw Huffman at the sugar camp, she knew he had not done it alone. And she would bet that it had not been his idea.

In his soft, deep voice, Huffman told Max and Boucher how he had met Beth Morton after the Brenners had ordered him to leave their home.

"I was going to drive all the way to the east coast," he said. "Look for work. Maybe on an oil rig." But Beth Morton changed his plans for him.

"How did you meet her?" Max asked.

"I was in my truck," Huffman said. "At a stoplight. I heard the car next to me sound its horn. I looked over, and this woman was smiling at me. Then she waved for me to pull over, and I did."

He said she asked if he had a job. When he told her he didn't, she said she needed someone to do yard work at her house.

"Said she'd pay me as much as I'd make on an oil rig," Huffman said. "Gave me money to get a motel room instead of sleeping in my truck." He ducked his head and smiled. "When she said she'd come and check my room, make sure I was set up good, well..."

"There was more to it than cutting grass," Max said.

Huffman nodded. "Driving all the way to the coast didn't sound like such a good idea after that."

Bob Morton met him two days later. "He didn't like me much from the get-go," Huffman said. "Guess he kinda knew what his wife was up to. Weren't the first time, way I saw it. Her gettin' a young guy like me to keep around." He looked at Max and Boucher. "Know what I'm saying?"

Max nodded.

Boucher said in an angry voice, "Keep talking."

The next time Huffman showed up, he heard Morton tell Beth he did not want *that dumb hick* around the house. Huffman said he could hear them screaming at each other while he was in the yard. Beth said Huffman would leave over her dead body. In reply Bob said, *So you want me to do to you what you did to Frank Higgs?*

"She'd told her husband about Higgs one night when she was drunk and mad at him," Huffman said. "Told him what she'd done to her first husband. How she gave him something besides the pills for his heart. And how he kept tryin' to get out of the pool. She'd keep pushing him with the pole."

Boucher looked at Max and said, "Does anyone else know about this?"

Max said, "Yes."

Boucher looked at her with his eyes wide and his mouth open.

Max ignored him. "Why would she tell this to Bob?" she asked Huffman.

"She'd be drunk and angry. He'd tell her to stop fooling around with guys. Guys like me. So she'd brag about what she could do. About what she had done." Huffman lowered his head into his hands.

"Keep going," Max said. She glanced at Boucher. His mouth was closed, but he was still glaring at her.

Huffman heard Morton say that if Beth didn't get rid of Ted, he would tell the police about Higgs's death. "He said they'd charge her with murdering that

Higgs guy," Huffman said. "She told him there was no proof, they'd never believe him. She'd say they were both drunk and that he was making it up. She'd had him cremated, her first husband. He'd died of a heart attack, that's what the corner had said. That's what was on the record. Death by heart attack and no body to check. So where was the proof? But I think it still scared her."

The next day Beth told her husband she would stop seeing Huffman. She said she was sorry she had upset him and that she'd sent Huffman away. She and Bob would plan a great night together on Saturday and renew their love for each other. Then she told Huffman not to come back to the house until she called him.

"Don't think he believed her," Huffman said. "Her husband, I mean. Who would? But he went along with it. Maybe because he loved her. Maybe because he wanted to." He gave a short laugh, more of a bark. "Maybe he was just stupid."

Beth called Huffman at the motel and told him to be at her house at 10 o'clock Saturday night. "I didn't know what she was up to," he said. "I didn't really want to go. But Beth, when she says to do somethin', you tend to do it. Like a fool, I went. I had no idea what she planned to do. I swear."

Later he learned that Beth had cooked a special dinner for herself and Bob. After dinner she mixed drinks for them. "The way she mixed them," Huffman said, "the only one who'd get drunk would be her husband."

When Huffman arrived, Bob was passed out on the sofa. Beth told Huffman she had told Bob she planned to leave him. "Said she'd be with me, just the two of us. That's what she told me."

Her husband's reaction, Beth said to Huffman, was to explode in anger. "He told her if she did that he'd shoot us both, Beth and me," Huffman said. "She told me, *He's got a gun, a big one*. She said it was in the house, and she couldn't find it. She told me when he woke up he would get it and kill her and me."

Huffman put his head in his hands. "I said, *Let's go, let's get out of here*. But she said, *No, he'd track us down, he'd find us*. There was only one thing we could do, she said, and she'd do it if I would just help her. That's all. Help her."

"And you did," Max said.

"Not at first. I kept saying we should call the police. She said we couldn't because Bob knew things about her that she didn't want the police to know."

"What did she mean by that?" Boucher asked. He had stopped staring at Max.

"About her first husband," Huffman said. "How he died."

Max spoke, and her voice was soft, almost sympathetic. "Why not call and tell us what was going on? Why not just walk away and let us know?"

Huffman thought about that. Then he said, "I can't explain it except that she was, um..." He started over. "She was wild in bed, and she said she would give me things. She said we would live in Muskoka, her and me, in that big house on the hill. I like this town. I wanted to stay here. But I told her I couldn't kill anybody. And then..." He closed his eyes, shook his head. "She said if I didn't help her, she would do it herself. If she was caught, she would say I did it. That she had gotten away with one and she could get away with another. Murder, she meant. If I helped her, she would never forget it, she..." He stopped for a moment.

"She loved me. She was doing this for me. It would take just minutes to do. *Let's get it over with*, she said." He began to cry. "So I did. I helped her. We did it, both of us. I still can't believe it, but we did it."

Max had heard it before from other murderers. One minute he can't believe he could kill someone. The next minute he's killing that person. Another minute later he can't believe what he just did.

They put a rope around his neck and each pulled on an end. Beth had worked out the details. When her husband stopped struggling, they took off his clothes and carried his naked body to a freezer in the garage. Beth said she would wait a few days before reporting him missing. "She said we should let the cops look for him," Huffman said. "After a week or so they would give up. Then we would carry the body up north and leave it deep in the bush. *Let the animals take care of him.*

That's what she said. She took over, and I let her. We spent the next two days together, mostly in bed. She kept telling me all the things we would do, all the places we would go. And I believed her." The tears had dried. "Because I wanted to."

On the second night, Beth said she didn't like keeping Bob's body in the house. They would move it and the freezer. Then she would report him missing. Together they loaded the freezer with the corpse inside onto Huffman's truck.

"She had worked everything out," he said. "I had told her about the old sugar camp. She said that's where I should stay until the police stopped looking for Bob. But there was no electric power there. We couldn't leave the body in the freezer like that…"

"So you stole the generator from the Brenners," Max said.

Huffman nodded.

He lived at the camp for a week. He would wake at night to hear the generator and freezer humming. Beth brought him a sleeping bag, camp stove and fishing rod. Some nights she stayed with him, and they shared the sleeping bag. Back at the house she cleaned the garage and painted the floor where the freezer had sat for years. Now there was no sign of it.

Two nights ago Huffman woke up. He was sure that he could hear Bob's voice coming from the freezer, screaming to be let out.

"I'd done the dumbest thing in my life when I helped kill him," Huffman said. "And I did the bravest thing I ever did when I opened the freezer. And took him out."

He put Bob in the truck under a blanket. Then, in the dead of night, he drove into town. "I didn't want animals to get him like Beth had said. So I put him in a ditch where he would be found. And drove away."

"And took the generator back," Max said.

Huffman nodded.

"What were you going to do with the freezer?"

"Take it apart piece by piece. Put the pieces in the back of the truck and head for the east coast," he said. "Drive on backroads and dump a piece every couple of miles. But I needed money for gas and stuff."

"So you asked Beth," Max said.

"Yeah."

"And when you asked her for money, she told you to get lost. She didn't need you anymore."

Huffman looked at her. "How'd you know?"

They put Huffman back in his cell. Boucher drove to Sunset Hill to arrest

Beth Morton for murder. Max said nothing when he left.

Boucher called Max after he arrived at Beth's house. "She's not here," he said. "There's no car in the garage. I'd say she left in a hurry. Any idea where we can look for her?"

Max said, "As a matter of fact, I do."

———

An hour later Boucher sat at Max's desk, sipping coffee. A slice of Margie's apple coffee cake was in front of him. Max was silent, keeping busy, telling herself not to feel smug.

Margie took a call from the Toronto police and handed the receiver to Boucher. He spoke a few words, gave the phone back to Margie and looked at Max. "You were right," he said. "The woman at the art gallery took the officers to a back room.

Beth Morton was hiding there. She's in custody. Ms. Morton, that is." He ate some cake and then said, "How did you know she would be at that art gallery? Who is this woman she went to? Where did you get all this info on your own?"

Max was about to speak when Henry leaned into her office. "Take a look outside," he said. "Nicest sight I've seen in weeks."

Max and PC 1st Class Ronald Boucher turned to look out the window. The sun was about to set in a clear, blue sky.

"Weather people say it'll be in the high twenties tomorrow," Henry said. "Gonna stay there all week. I think summer's found us at last."

"Such a pretty sight," Max said. She pictured herself on the porch of her cottage that evening, sipping tea with Geegee. Just wait, she thought, until Geegee finds out she helped solve a murder case. Because she had, with her comment about the generator.

"Hello there." It was Boucher. He had been watching her sit in silence. When Max turned to him he said, "I'll ask you again. Who is the woman at the art gallery? And how did you know Beth Morton would go there to hide from us? And what else do you know about her first husband?"

Max smiled. "Have another piece of Margie's coffee cake," she said. Summer was here for sure. So was something else. "This is a really good story."

Boucher said, "I don't have time for stories."

Was that a sneer in his voice? It sounded like it.

"All right," Max said with a smile. "Then how about a lesson? On how to solve a murder?"

PREVIEW OF
MURDER AMONG THE PINES,
THE NEXT MAXINE BENSON MYSTERY

Max stepped from the cruiser at 5:37 AM and paused to write the time in her notebook. She had parked on a paved area near the water. Across the inlet the Ainslic Inn rose seven stories high. The inn rarely had a vacant room on weekends. It had been a success since it opened two years ago. Picnic tables were set among pine trees that lined a stone path leading to the inlet of the lake. During the day, many guests bought box lunches at the inn and carried them along the shore to the grove of pines, a ten-minute walk.

The sun rising behind Granite Mountain shone on the far shore of the lake. The inn still sat in shadow. In the low light she saw the body floating a few metres from shore. It was easy to see the long dark hair. It was almost as easy to see that the woman was Lana Jewel Laverne Parker.

Max glanced at the people standing around her. A middle-aged man and woman in tracksuits were arm in arm, the woman's head on the man's shoulder. Max was sure they were the ones who first had seen the body and reported it to the desk clerk at the inn. Behind them stood Perry Ahenakew, a First Nations artist who had a small studio down the road. She knew him as a gentle man, a skilled artist. He nodded back at her. Not far behind him was a man named Bucky, who ran a towing service on the highway. Near him, a white-haired man held back his dog on its leash. Behind him a younger man in a light jacket stood shaking his head as though in sorrow.

"All of you," Max called to them. She raised an arm and pointed to the paved area where she had parked her cruiser. "This is a crime scene. Go to the parking area and wait there. Someone will talk to you later."

The group shuffled away just as Henry pulled up to park his cruiser behind hers. "Bring a blanket with you," she called to him. "Keep these people back and get the names of whoever called it in. Then contact the provincials in Cranston. Tell them to send the coroner." She pulled a pair of rubber gloves from her tunic, put them on, and waded into the lake. She shivered as the cold water reached to her waist.

The woman was floating face down. She wore a black t-shirt and jeans. When Max turned her over she could see, even in the dim light, that the victim had been beaten. She gently pulled the body toward the shore. In her years as a police officer in

Toronto she had seen several dead bodies. This one did not shock her, but it made her feel guilty and sad. Guilty that she had said unkind things about the woman. Sad that her young life had been taken in such a brutal way.

JOHN LAWRENCE REYNOLDS has had thirty works of fiction and nonfiction published. His work has earned two Arthur Ellis Awards for Best Mystery Novel, a National Business Book Award and a CBC Bookie Award. His bestselling book *Shadow People*, tracing the development and influence of secret societies through history, was published in fourteen countries and twelve languages. He has also authored several business and investment books, including the bestselling *Naked Investor* and its sequel, *The Skeptical Investor*, as well as his assessment of the 2008–2009 global financial crisis, *Bubbles, Bankers & Bailouts*. His first book for this series, *A Murder for Max*, introduced Maxine Benson to Rapid Reads. He lives in Burlington, Ontario, with his wife, Judy. For more information, visit www.wryter.ca.

READ THE FIRST BOOK IN THE
MAXINE BENSON
MYSTERY SERIES

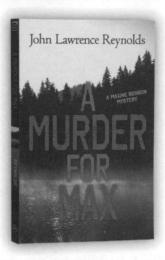

Escaping the pressures of big-city policing, Maxine Benson is happy to be appointed police chief in the resort town of Port Ainslie. Max's biggest challenge is to overcome skepticism at her ability to deal with major crimes—like the murder of Billy Ray Edwards. Few people mourn Billy Ray's passing. He was a bully and was also intent on derailing the biggest development project in the town's history. But murder's murder, and Max is ready to solve it on her own and prove her worth to the townspeople. And maybe even to herself.

> "Readers will hope that there will be a long
> line of Maxine Benson mysteries."
> — *CM Reviews*

ORCA BOOK PUBLISHERS
www.orcabook.com